If You Give a Mouse a Cookie

If You Give a

Mouse a Cookie

Laura Joffe Numeroff
ILLUSTRATED BY Felicia Bond

HarperCollins*Publishers*

For Florence & William Numeroff,
the two best parents anyone could
ever possibly want!   L. J. N.

For Stephen   F. B.

HarperCollins*Publishers*

First published in the USA in 1985
by HarperCollins*Publishers, Inc.*
First published in Australia in 2002
by HarperCollins*Publishers* Pty Limited
A member of the HarperCollins*Publishers* (Australia) Pty Limited Group

25 Ryde Road, Pymble, NSW 2073, Australia
31 View Road, Glenfield, Auckland 10, New Zealand

ISBN 0 7322 7410 9

Manufactured in China

1 2 3 4 5   01 02 03 04

If you give a mouse a cookie,

he's going to ask for a glass of milk.

When you give him the milk,

he'll probably ask you for a straw.

When he's finished, he'll ask for a napkin.

Then he'll want to look in a mirror
to make sure he doesn't
have a milk moustache.

When he looks into the mirror,

he might notice his hair needs a trim.

So he'll probably ask
for a pair of nail scissors.

When he's finished giving himself a trim,
he'll want a broom to sweep up.

He'll start sweeping.

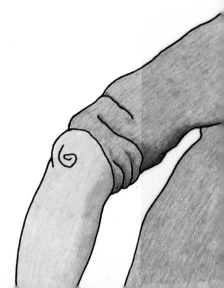

He might get carried away and
sweep every room in the house.

He may even end up washing the floors as well!

When he's done,
he'll probably want to take a nap.

You'll have to fix up a little box for him
with a blanket and a pillow.

He'll crawl in,
make himself comfortable
and fluff the pillow a few times.

He'll probably ask you to read him a story.

So you'll read to him from one of your books,
and he'll ask to see the pictures.

When he looks at the pictures,
he'll get so excited he'll want to draw
one of his own. He'll ask for paper and crayons.

He'll draw a picture.

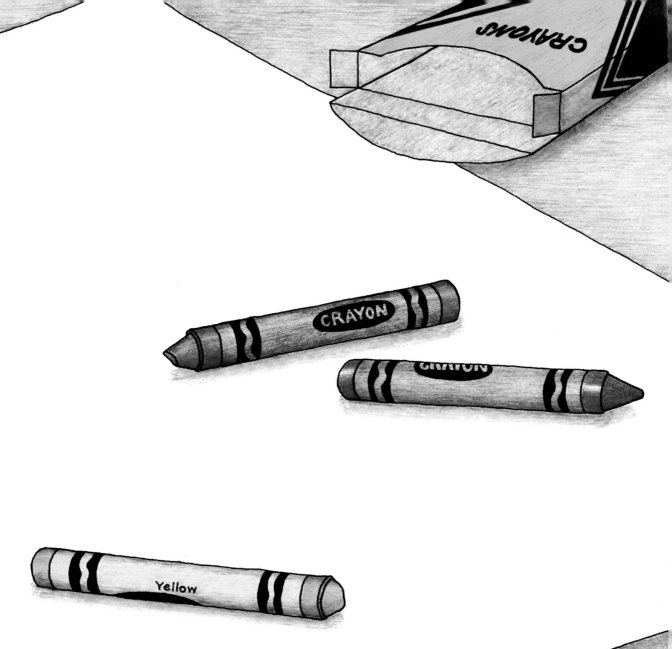

When the picture is finished,

he'll want to sign his name

with a pen.

Then he'll want to hang
his picture on your
refrigerator.

Which means he'll need

Sticky tape.

He'll hang up his drawing
and stand back to look at it.

Looking at the refrigerator
will remind him that

he's thirsty.

So . . .

he'll ask for a glass of milk.

And chances are if he asks for
a glass of milk,

he's going to want a cookie to go with it.